Carmen
the Cheerleading
Fairy

Carmen
the Cheerleading
Fairy

By Daisy Meadows

ORCHARD

www.orchardseriesbooks.co.uk

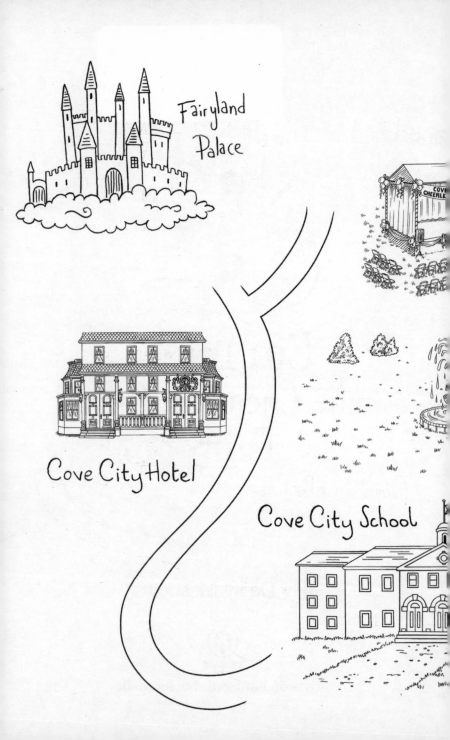

Fairyland Palace

Cove City Hotel

Cove City School

For Luke and Lucy, my reasons to cheer

Special thanks to
Shannon Penney

ORCHARD BOOKS

First published in Great Britain in 2021 by The Watts Publishing Group

1 3 5 7 9 10 8 6 4 2

© 2022 Rainbow Magic Limited.
© 2022 HIT Entertainment Limited.
Illustrations © 2022 The Watts Publishing Group Limited.

HIT entertainment

A CIP catalogue record for this book is available from the British Library.

ISBN 978 1 40836 452 9

Printed and bound in Great Britain by Clays Ltd, Elcograf S.p.A

FSC
www.fsc.org

MIX
Paper from
responsible sources
FSC® C104740

The paper and board used in this book are made from wood from responsible sources.

Orchard Books
An imprint of Hachette Children's Group
Part of The Watts Publishing Group Limited
Carmelite House, 50 Victoria Embankment, London EC4Y 0DZ

An Hachette UK Company
www.hachette.co.uk
www.hachettechildrens.co.uk

andstand
Jack Frost's Ice Castle
Gymnasium
Gymnasium
Cove City Park

Contents

Story One:
Pom-Pom Problems

Story Two:
Picture Perfect

Story Three:
Megaphone Madness

Jack Frost's Ode

You might think that you have a reason to cheer
But I'll make your good feelings – poof! – disappear.
Magic pom-pom, hair bow and megaphone too –
They're mine now! No cheerleading magic for you.

I'm sick of the cheer, the sunshine and smiles.
I have to admit, they're just not my style.
So go on and try all your flips and your tumbles,
But now, thanks to me, you're going to stumble!

Story One
Pom-Pom Problems

Chapter One
Perilous Practice

"I can't believe we're finally here!"
Kirsty Tate cried, grinning. "I've always
dreamed about taking part in a real
cheerleading competition."

Her best friend, Rachel Walker,
squeezed her hand. "I can believe it!
You and your squad have worked really

hard. I'm so glad I got to come along to watch you compete!"

The girls linked arms and skipped across the huge lawn in the middle of the Cove College school. They'd come to Cove City with Kirsty's parents for the big Junior Cheerleading Competition that weekend! It was Kirsty's first year

on a squad, and this was their very
first competition. Rachel and Kirsty
had only just arrived, but the weekend
already felt magical!

"Looks like the competition is in there,"
Mr Tate called from behind the girls,
pointing to a large brick building on one
corner of the lawn. The archway over the
door read 'COVE COLLEGE GYMNASIUM'.

Kirsty smiled and pulled Rachel over
to the brick building.

"Is the rest of your squad meeting you
here?" Rachel asked, pulling the gym
door open.

"Yup! It's our last practice before the
competition tomorrow," Kirsty said,
peering around the massive gym in awe.
"Though I'm not sure how I'll ever find
them. This place is huge!"

Girls and boys were scattered all over the gym. Some were stretching and warming up, while others chatted excitedly. Colourful mats covered the floor, and Rachel and Kirsty could see piles of pom-poms and stacks of megaphones over by the benches.

"Kirsty!" a voice suddenly called. A girl with a curly black ponytail ran up and

gave Kirsty a hug. "Can you believe all this?"

Kirsty shook her head, smiling. "I guess we need a big gym to hold this much cheer!" She turned to Rachel. "Rachel, this is my friend Sunny. She's the captain of our squad."

"I can't wait to see your routine!" Rachel said, waving as Kirsty and Sunny ran off to join their teammates.

"Come on, Rachel," Mrs Tate said. "Let's find a spot on the benches to watch them practise."

From the benches, Rachel, Mr Tate and Mrs Tate had a perfect view of the whole gym. There was an awful lot to see! Rachel counted ten different squads practising before she turned her attention back to Kirsty's team.

"OK, let's go!"
Sunny cried.
She and a
boy with
spiky brown
hair led the
squad in
their opening
cheer. Rachel
couldn't help
noticing that
they were all
out of sync — some
of the kids were forgetting the words,
and others were doing the wrong arm
movements.

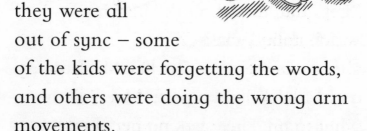

*Maybe they just need a minute to
get warmed up,* Rachel thought,
frowning.

Kirsty and her friends started to look more and more frustrated as they worked their way through the routine. Things weren't getting better! One girl fell during a simple jump, and another accidentally kicked one of her teammates in the face while doing a cartwheel! Their coach, Mrs Gold, stood to one side, shaking her head in confusion.

"I've never seen them make so many mistakes," Mrs Tate murmured. "What could be going on?"

"I don't know," Mr Tate said. "But they're not the only ones ..."

He was right! Rachel had been so busy watching Kirsty's squad that she hadn't noticed, but all around the gym, kids were tripping and slipping through their routines. Everyone was forgetting moves, stumbling during tumbles and dropping pom-poms. What a mess!

Rachel looked back at Kirsty's squad just in time to see them form a pyramid. *Whew*, Rachel thought, watching Sunny climb into place on the very top, *at least that turned out OK!* But suddenly, the pyramid began to wobble and sway – and then it collapsed!

Rachel gasped, watching Kirsty
and her teammates topple to the mat.
Luckily, no one seemed to be hurt – but
something was definitely not right . . .

Chapter Two
A Magic Mission

Just then, a flash of light caught Rachel's eye. She blinked. What was that?

There it is again! she thought, spotting a twinkle in a nearby pile of pom-poms. She had to get a closer look!

"If it's all right, I thought I'd take a walk around the gym and check out

some of the other squads," she said to
Mr and Mrs Tate.

Kirsty's parents nodded. "Of course,
Rachel," Mr Tate said, with a smile.
"Just make sure none of those crazy
cheerleaders tumble into you!"

Rachel laughed and headed down
the benches, keeping her eyes on
the pile of pom-poms. As she tiptoed
closer, she saw the twinkling light
again. This time, she could also see what
was causing it − a tiny shimmering
fairy, nestled in the pom-poms! She
had a dark brown ponytail and wore
a colorful cheerleading uniform.

"Hi!" Rachel whispered with a grin,
sitting down next to the pile. "I'm
Rachel. Is everything OK?"

The fairy looked up at her in surprise, and then she smiled in relief. "Oh, Rachel, I was hoping you and Kirsty would find me! I've heard all about  you." She smoothed her skirt and suddenly looked sad. "I'm Carmen the Cheerleading Fairy. I'm sorry that I'm not full of more cheer right now – my magic objects are missing. Without them, cheerleading everywhere is a total disaster!"

"Let me guess," Rachel said. "Jack Frost has been up to no good?"

Carmen nodded and crossed her arms angrily. "Of course! He's such an icy old grouch, I shouldn't be surprised that he's taking it out on me."

Rachel glanced around the gym. "So that's why this practice is such a mess!"

"It's awful, isn't it?" Carmen sighed. "These children have worked so hard to get to this competition, and now nothing is going right. I'm afraid someone might get seriously hurt

if I don't find my magic objects — and fast!"

Nearby, a girl fell to the mat with a hard *thud*.

Rachel flinched. Carmen was right, they had to fix this!

"What do your objects look like?" she asked Carmen. "I'll help you find them."

"Oh, thank you!" Carmen cheered, clapping her hands and grinning. "I was looking in this pile of pom-poms, hoping to find my magic pom-pom. It controls athleticism, and helps people nail their moves and cheerleading routines. But I don't see it anywhere!" She shrugged.

"Jack Frost and his goblins are very good at hiding things," Rachel explained.

"I'm also missing
my magic hair
bow, which
controls
teamwork,
helping people
work together
and support one
another," Carmen
said. "And my
magic megaphone

is missing, too! That one controls
confidence and positive attitudes, helping
cheerleaders to believe in themselves and
look on the bright side."

Suddenly, a loud whistle echoed
through the gym. Practice was over! All
of the squads, including Kirsty's, looked
worried as they gathered their things.

"Here, you can hide in my shirt pocket," Rachel whispered, holding her pocket open while Carmen fluttered into it. "Let's fill Kirsty in, and then we'll look for your magical objects."

Carmen looked up and gave her a half-hearted smile.

Rachel waved to Kirsty, and her friend walked over, hanging her head.

"That was just awful!" Kirsty moaned. "If we perform like that tomorrow, we're going to be the laughing stock of the whole competition."

Rachel gave Kirsty a hug, and then pulled her out of sight behind a rolled-up tumbling mat. "I know you're feeling down," she said, "but this might cheer you up!"

Carmen peeked out of Rachel's

pocket and used her wand to send
a swirl of sparkles into the air. "Hi,
Kirsty! I'm Carmen the Cheerleading
Fairy."

Kirsty gasped and her face lit up. "Oh,
Carmen, I'm so happy to see you!"

Rachel quickly explained how Jack

Frost had stolen Carmen's magical objects.

"So that's why everyone's routines are going so badly!" Kirsty cried.

"Right," Carmen said with a nod, raising her arms above her head. "Gimme an M! Gimme an E! Gimme an S! Gimme another S! What's that spell? MESS!"

Rachel squeezed Kirsty's hand. "If we can find Carmen's magic objects before tomorrow, maybe we'll be able to save the competition!"

Kirsty jumped to her feet. "There's no time to lose!" Then she frowned. "But where do we start?"

Chapter Three
Terrific Tumblers!

Kirsty, Rachel and Carmen scanned the busy gym. There was no sign of Carmen's magic objects, or naughty goblins, anywhere!

"We're never going to find anything in here," Rachel said. "It's too crowded."

Kirsty looked thoughtful. "You're right.

Let's look around the hallways until the gym clears out." She flagged down her parents and got permission to explore, and then the girls slipped into the hall. Carmen ducked safely inside Rachel's pocket again.

After being in the loud gym, the hallway seemed extra quiet. Rachel and Kirsty's footsteps echoed as they walked.

Suddenly, Carmen tugged on Rachel's pocket. "Do you hear that?"

Both girls froze, listening carefully. Carmen was right! There was something happening

up ahead, around a corner. Rachel and Kirsty looked at each other in excitement. Could it be . . . goblins?

Together they raced down the hall, careful to make as little noise as possible. When they reached the corner, they screeched to a stop and peeked around it.

Both girls' jaws dropped! There, in the adjacent hallway, was a whole group of goblins performing an elaborate tumbling routine! They did cartwheels, handsprings and flips. Flying through the air as if they had springs on their hands and feet.

"They're amazing!" Kirsty whispered.

Rachel nodded, her eyes wide. "And they never seem to get tired."

It was true! The goblins tumbled over

and over, never stumbling or pausing
for a break. They weren't getting worn
out at all – and they were clearly having
a great time!

Carmen tugged on Rachel's ponytail.
"That's because they have my magic
pom-pom!" she whispered, clapping her
hands in excitement. "Remember, it helps
cheerleaders with their routines. That's

why the goblins are perfecting so many
tumbling moves in a row."

She pointed to a trio of goblins nearby.
One of them held a pair of pom-poms
while two others tossed him high into
the air ... and one of the pom-poms was
sparkling with fairy magic!

"See? There it is!" Carmen shouted.

Kirsty almost let out a triumphant cheer, but Rachel clapped a hand over her mouth just in time.

"Sorry," Kirsty whispered with a giggle. "I got a little carried away!"

Rachel grinned. "Let's come up with a plan for getting the pom-pom back *before* the goblins notice us," she said.

Rachel and Kirsty sat down and put their heads together, whispering and thinking hard. But they hadn't gotten very far when Carmen fluttered up out of Rachel's pocket, peeked around the corner and darted back faster than lightning. She landed on Kirsty's shoulder, looking worried.

"Oh no! We have to go, quickly!" she cried, pointing.

When Kirsty and Rachel peeked around the corner again, they saw what Carmen was fretting about. The goblins were still tumbling like cheerleading champions — right through the door at the end of the hallway!

They were heading outside . . . and they were taking Carmen's magic pom-pom with them!

Chapter Four
Cheerleading Chaos!

"Don't let them get away!" Carmen cried.

Rachel and Kirsty jumped to their feet and dashed down the hallway after the goblins. Carmen followed Kirsty closely, her ponytail blowing behind her. The door was just swinging shut as they

reached it and barrelled through.

Both girls screeched to a halt as the door slammed behind them. They looked around. Which way had the goblins gone?

"There!" Kirsty cried, pointing to a familiar flash of green disappearing around one side of the gym. "They're heading for Cove City park!"

Rachel followed her friend as fast as she could run, trying to keep her eye on the goblin with the magic pom-pom. "Good thing the goblins are wearing clothes.

Anyone who spots them will probably just think they're kids!"

When they rounded the corner, the girls had no trouble spotting the goblins. The tiny troublemakers were causing quite a scene! They tumbled across the paths, causing students to stumble and bikers to veer onto the grass. They somersaulted through flowerbeds, leaving a trail of dirty destruction behind them. They even cartwheeled through the fountain at the centre of the park, splashing everyone nearby!

"This is chaos!" Kirsty said, shaking her head. "We have to stop them before someone gets hurt."

Carmen tickled Kirsty's ear to get her attention. "Luckily, it looks like the

goblins are finally ready for a break."

Sure enough, the goblins had flopped down on the grass, tossing their pompoms down beside them. They stretched out and chatted excitedly.

"Did you see that amazing flip I did in the fountain?"

"That was nothing compared to my

seventeen backsprings in a row!"

"I out-tumbled all of you, no contest!"

Rachel rolled her eyes. The goblins
could always find something to brag
about! That gave her an idea ...

She whispered her plan to Kirsty
and Carmen. Once Carmen had
tucked herself safely back into Rachel's

shirt pocket, the two girls cheerfully approached the goblins.

"Wow!" Kirsty exclaimed. "You're all amazing tumblers!"

The goblins sat up tall, grinning proudly.

"I wish I could cheer like you," Rachel added wistfully. "Could you teach us some moves?"

"Sure!" the goblins cried in unison, jumping to their feet.

A goblin grabbed the girls' hands and led them to a wide-open area of grass.

"First, you need to master a back handspring." He demonstrated the move, making it look easy. Then he and his friends helped Kirsty, then Rachel, making sure they didn't fall as each girl gave it a try.

"Wow, that was fun!" Rachel said, with a laugh. She'd never done a back handspring before! And she had to admit – the goblins were good teachers!

"Can you teach us a cheer sequence?" Kirsty asked the goblins.

Another goblin stepped forward.

"Absolutely! Here, you'll need these."
He handed each girl a set of
pom-poms.

Rachel gasped and then coughed,
trying to cover her surprise. One of the
pom-poms in her hand sparkled and
shimmered.

She couldn't believe it. The goblin had
handed her the magic pom-pom!

Chapter Five
A Reason to Cheer

"Ready? Let's go!" the goblin cried, raising his pom-poms into the air.

Rachel waved her pom-poms overhead, winking at Kirsty as the magic pom-pom glittered in the sunlight. She heard a squeal of excitement from her pocket. Carmen had spotted the magic pom-pom, too!

The goblin began a cheer sequence, and his friends scrambled to their feet to join in. As Rachel lowered her pom-poms to clap them together, she brought the magic pom-pom close to her shirt pocket. Carmen reached out to touch it, and it immediately shrank back to fairy-size!

"Got it!" Carmen cheered happily. In the blink of an eye, she twirled up in the air and disappeared in a shower of sparkles, taking the magic pom-pom with her!

Rachel and Kirsty tried their best to pretend that nothing had

happened, finishing out the cheer sequence enthusiastically.

When they were done, the goblin who had had the magic pom-pom turned to face them. "Not bad, for beginners," he said. "Of course, you'll need to keep practising if you want to be as good as me, but that's—"

Suddenly, he froze. He stared at Rachel, who held a pom-pom in one hand and nothing in the other.

"Hey . . . what happened to your other pom-pom?" he asked slowly.

Rachel shrugged. She didn't want to lie, so she chose her words carefully. "I don't think that pom-pom belonged to you, did it?"

The goblin who had shown them the back handspring stepped forward,

peering around frantically. "Wait! No! Did you give her the MAGIC pom-pom?" He smacked his forehead with one big green hand. "And now it's missing? Jack Frost is never going to let us hear the end of this!"

The other goblin snorted. "This never would have happened in the first place if

you hadn't been such a show-off!"

"Me?" the first goblin cried. "I'm not the one who handed the magic pom-pom to a total stranger!"

As the other goblins jumped into the argument, shouting and stomping their feet, Rachel and Kirsty slipped away unnoticed.

"That was a lucky break," Kirsty said, once they were a safe distance away.

Rachel laughed. "You're telling me!

"I can't believe he handed Carmen's magic pom-pom right to me."

"And now that Carmen's pom-pom has been returned to Fairyland, our routines should go much more smoothly." Kirsty sighed with relief. "I don't think I can handle another toppling pyramid!"

The girls headed back to the gym to meet up with Kirsty's parents.

"So what's next?" Rachel asked, linking arms with her best friend.

Kirsty pulled open the gym door. "Well, it's time to check in to the hotel and get dinner with my squad," she said. "I can't wait for you to meet everyone! But more importantly . . ."

". . . we have to find Carmen's other magical objects!" Rachel finished.

There was no time to waste. If the girls didn't find Carmen's magic hair bow and megaphone before the morning, Kirsty's first big competition was going to be a big disaster!

Story Two
Picture Perfect

Chapter Six
Teamwork Trouble

"Yum!" said Rachel, rubbing her stomach with satisfaction. "That dinner was so good! I hadn't realised how hungry I was."

"Me neither," Kirsty said, smiling. She dropped her voice to a whisper. "I guess chasing goblins around all afternoon really helps work up an appetite!"

Rachel laughed. Kirsty was right – running after silly goblins was hard work! As her laugh faded, she glanced around at the rest of Kirsty's squad. They were all walking to the Cove City Hotel after eating dinner together, and there wasn't a smile to be seen! All of the kids looked awfully gloomy ...

"Here we are," said Mrs Gold, the squad's coach. She pointed to a large, old, fancy-looking building up ahead. Lanterns flickered on either side of the entrance, and a wrought iron sign over the door read 'COVE CITY HOTEL'.

Even though they were feeling gloomy, the kids on Kirsty's squad couldn't help looking at the hotel in awe.

"Wow," Sunny said. "I can't believe we get to stay here!"

"We'll go grab the bags from our car and check in," Mrs Tate told Rachel and Kirsty. "Why don't you two have a look around? We'll meet you in the lobby in a little bit."

"Thanks, Mum!" Kirsty said. This was just the opportunity they needed to explore. Maybe they would even track down another one of Carmen the Cheerleading Fairy's missing objects – if they were lucky!

Kirsty turned to the rest of her squad. Everyone was heading inside and up to their rooms. "Goodnight, everyone. See you tomorrow for the big day!"

The other kids all tried to smile and wave as they disappeared through the front doors. Kirsty paused outside the hotel and sighed.

"Everyone has been so snappy and impatient all afternoon. Our squad usually gets along so well! At this rate, we won't be working together very well for tomorrow's competition." She buried her face in her hands. "All our hard work could be for nothing!"

Rachel gave her friend a hug. "This is because Carmen's magic hair bow is still missing," she said. "It controls teamwork, remember? We just have to find it, and then everything will go back to normal!"

Kirsty took a deep breath. "You're right." She stood up tall and squeezed Rachel's hand. "Let's go inside. Hopefully some magic will find us soon – we don't have much time!"

Together the girls pulled open the large front doors of the hotel and stepped into the ornate lobby. A big wooden desk stood off to one side, lit with old lamps and some flickering candles. Huge, overstuffed chairs around the lobby were filled with all kinds of visitors, chatting and relaxing. Jazz music played on some speakers, and a crystal chandelier glittered overhead.

"This place is amazing!" Rachel said, turning in a slow circle and trying to take it all in.

Kirsty nodded, but didn't say anything.
She was too busy studying the crystal
chandelier.

Rachel watched her friend curiously.
"It's a nice chandelier ..." she commented
after a moment.

"It's not just that," Kirsty whispered. "Look over on the left side. Doesn't it seem . . . *extra* sparkly?"

Rachel squinted, then gasped. Sure enough, there was a glimmering figure perched on one arm of the chandelier. "Carmen!" Rachel cried.

Quick as a flash, the tiny fairy darted down and ducked into Kirsty's tote. Fortunately, no one in the busy lobby seemed to notice!

Carmen peeked over the edge of the bag and grinned at the girls. "Hello

again! I hope you're not too tired from your long day, because I can sense my magic hair bow nearby."

"We were hoping you'd say that!" Kirsty whispered.

"This old hotel has a lot of nooks and crannies," Rachel said. "The goblins could be anywhere ..."

"Then we'd better get started!" Carmen cheered.

Chapter Seven
Hotel High Jinks

Rachel, Kirsty, and Carmen looked around the crowded lobby. There was a lot going on, but they didn't notice anything unusual or goblin-like.

"Let's pick a hallway and start exploring," Kirsty suggested, pointing to a hall that led off the main lobby.

Carmen ducked down inside Kirsty's tote again, and the three friends set off. No sooner had they left the noisy lobby than they heard the *ding* of an arriving elevator up ahead. The doors slid open and the girls jumped back! They'd almost been run over by a group of kids leaping and

tumbling out of the elevator at full speed!

"Whoa!" Rachel cried. "Those kids are acting crazy!"

Kirsty watched the group somersault down the hallway, frowning. "Those aren't kids . . . they're goblins!"

A tiny gasp came from inside Kirsty's bag. "After them!" Carmen cried.

Rachel and Kirsty raced down the hall as fast as their legs would take them, barely able to keep the tumbling goblins in sight as they went around corners and through doorways.

"Look, one of them is wearing the magic hair bow!" Rachel pointed out, before the goblins ran through a set of swinging doors.

The girls barreled through the doors after them and then stopped short.

They'd almost
run right into the
hotel's indoor
pool!

"That would
have been a very
*un*magical surprise,"
Kirsty muttered.

On the far side of the
pool, the goblins were
executing perfect
cheerleading tosses
and heaving their
teammates into
the water. Each goblin
landed with a huge *SPLASH*, soaking
the other swimmers and all the people
on the pool deck, too!

The girls watched as the goblin with

the hair bow sailed through the air, turning three impressive flips before cannonballing into the deep end.

Kirsty shook her head. "Those goblins are causing so much trouble!"

"That's true, but see how well they're working together?" Carmen pointed out. "That's because they have my magic hair bow." She blinked, squinting at the goblin who had just landed in the water. "Wait – where did it go?"

"There!" Rachel said, pointing to another goblin at the edge of the pool. "They're working together so well that they're also sharing the hair bow, and goblins never share!"

Suddenly, all of the goblins climbed out of the water and ran back through the swinging doors, leaving a slick trail behind them. Rachel and Kirsty followed, trying not to slip!

The goblins sped down the halls again, tossing the hair bow back and forth as they cartwheeled and flipped. When they reached the lobby, they all began to somersault in unison. They looked like a row of runaway bowling balls rolling through the crowd! People yelped and scattered in every direction.

"I can't keep track of which goblin has the hair bow," Rachel said, breathing hard as she ran.

"Me neither," said Kirsty, wiping her forehead. "At this rate, we'll never get it back!"

All at once, the goblins climbed to their

feet again and tumbled off down
another hallway, clapping
and cheering in perfect
unison.

"We're green!
We're mean!
We're a top-notch
team!
We'll cause more
trouble than you've
ever seen!"

Carmen peeked out
of Kirsty's bag and
sighed. "Well, they've
got that part right. If
we don't stop them soon,
they're going to cause a heap of
trouble not just here, but for cheerleaders
everywhere!"

Chapter Eight
Goblins Take the Cake

Rachel and Kirsty skidded around a corner and came to a sudden stop. The goblins had stopped too and they were standing right in front of the girls! Rachel and Kirsty didn't want to be spotted, so they quickly ducked behind a potted plant. Carmen fluttered silently out of Kirsty's tote and perched on one of the plant's wide leaves.

"What are they doing?" she whispered, peeking at the group of goblins.

Kirsty groaned. "I don't like the look of this," she said quietly. "Do you see what they're all huddled around?"

"Oh!" Rachel gasped. "It's a wedding cake!"

It was true!
The upper tiers
of a beautiful
white wedding
cake towered
above the
goblins' heads.
The cake was
covered with
frosting flowers and

the girls could see the small figures of a
bride and groom on the very top. The
goblins surrounded it, giggling gleefully
and licking their lips.

"That's the entrance to the ballroom,"
Kirsty said, pointing to the doors just
beyond the goblins. "And see the sign
over there? 'The Greene and Jones
Wedding'. There's a wedding reception
going on right now!"

Carmen frowned, crossing her arms.
"This time, the goblins have gone too
far! It's one thing to ruin the
cheerleading competition, but now
they're going to spoil a wedding, too?"
She stomped her foot, and the leaf
she was standing on bobbed up and
down. "What a bunch of greedy green
meanies!"

Just then, they
heard the goblin
with the hair
bow speak up.
"OK, team.
Here's what
we'll do: let's
form a goblin
pyramid. That
way, we can climb

up high and snag the delicious top of
the cake! That silly bride and groom will
never even miss it."

Rachel shook her head in disbelief. "Of
course they'll miss it; it's their wedding
cake!"

But the other goblins all nodded
enthusiastically, cheering, "Great idea!",
"Take the cake!" and "Goooo, team!"

They quieted down and listened as the
goblin with the hair bow told them how
to form the strongest, sturdiest pyramid.
Then they scrambled into position.
In no time, they began to form an
incredible goblin pyramid right there in
the hallway! Five goblins made the base
of the pyramid, then four on the next
level, three on the next level . . .

Kirsty, Rachel and Carmen all held
their breath as the pyramid grew taller
and taller. Before long, it was almost
as high as the towering cake! The
goblin with the hair bow nodded in
satisfaction, then got ready to begin his
climb. Rachel and Kirsty could see that
once he reached the top of the pyramid,
he'd be able to grab the top tier of the
cake easily!

Suddenly, Kirsty's face lit up. "Team huddle!" she whispered to Rachel and Carmen. The little fairy fluttered down to perch on Kirsty's shoulder, and Rachel leaned in close. "I have an idea," Kirsty went on. "But in order for it to work, we're going to need a little magic . . ."

Carmen grinned. "You're in luck, girls!" She held up her wand. "Magic happens to be my specialty."

Chapter Nine
Zipping and Zooming

Eyes twinkling, Rachel, Kirsty and Carmen crouched behind the potted plant and watched the goblin pyramid closely. The girls had to wait for just the right moment to put their plan into action!

The goblin with the hair bow climbed

confidently up each level of the pyramid, while his teammates cheered him on.

"You've got this!"

"Nearly there!"

"I can almost taste that cake now!"

As the goblin with the hair bow began to climb the uppermost level to take his place at the top, Kirsty gave Carmen a nod. The little fairy took a deep breath. "It's time, girls!"

Carmen waved her wand, and a twinkling of magic surrounded Kirsty and Rachel. In the blink of an eye, they both shrank down to fairy-size! Thin, sparkling wings appeared on each of their backs.

Kirsty fluttered her wings happily. "Being turned into a fairy is the best!"

"You bet it is!" Rachel smiled, flying

into the air and giving Carmen a high five. "Now let's take down that pyramid and get Carmen's bow back."

The three fairies darted out of hiding, and not a moment too soon! The goblin with the bow had just reached the very top of the pyramid, and he was about to

reach for the top of the cake.

"Hey!" Kirsty cried, zooming over to the goblins. "That cake isn't yours and neither is that bow on your head!"

The goblin with the bow scoffed. "Finders keepers!" His teammates all laughed and cheered.

Rachel landed on the goblin's big nose. "That's not how it works. An important part of cheerleading is being a good sport and playing fair."

She stomped her foot and the

84

goblin yelped, swatting her away with a wave of his hand.

"Get out of here, you pesky fairies!" he grumbled. "We've been working very hard and we're hungry. If you'll excuse us, now we have some cake to eat." He stretched out a hand towards the top tier of the wedding cake.

But before he could reach the cake, Rachel, Kirsty and Carmen began flying in circles around his head! They zipped and zoomed, dipped and dived. They couldn't get close enough to grab the magic bow, but they got just close enough to completely confuse and annoy the goblin!

"Stop that! Cut it out!" he cried, waving an arm to shoo them away.

The three friends flew expertly, dodging the goblin's flailing arms. They

continued to dart
around him like
pesky flies
and they
couldn't
help
giggling as
he got more
and more
annoyed!

"I mean
it!" the goblin
yelled, rising to
his knees and swatting at the fairies with
both green hands. He almost sent Kirsty
tumbling through the air with a wild
swing, but she dipped away just in time!
As she did, the goblin lost his balance
and fell to one side, landing on the two

goblins below him with a thud.

"Whoa!" they cried, startled. They
began to wobble, which set off a chain
reaction down the rest of the pyramid.
The whole thing started to sway!

Rachel, Kirsty and Carmen watched
from the air as the goblins all desperately

tried working together to regain their balance.

"Lean to the left!" one cried.

Another goblin shouted, "Nobody panic! Hold steady!"

But even teamwork magic couldn't save the pyramid. As the fairies looked on, the whole thing tilted, tipped and then came tumbling down!

Chapter Ten
Taking a Bow

"Ow!"

"Get off me!"

"Whose foot is in my face?!"

The toppled pyramid of goblins lay in a heap, grumbling and groaning. They pushed and shoved while some of the goblins climbed gingerly to their feet. The rest of the goblins were a tangled pile of arms and legs!

Fluttering in the air above, Kirsty noticed a familiar sparkle. The magic hair bow! The goblin wearing it had been trapped under some of his teammates when he fell. Luckily, his head and the hair bow were the only things sticking out of the goblin pileup. This was Kirsty's chance!

Zooming as fast as her wings would carry her, Kirsty made a beeline for the goblin and plucked the bow from his head. Standing on his forehead, she bent over so she could see his face – upside-down!

"Thank you!" she told him sweetly. "The true owner of this magic bow will be very happy to have it back."

The goblin glared at her. His green face turned a furious shade of red but there was nothing he could do! His

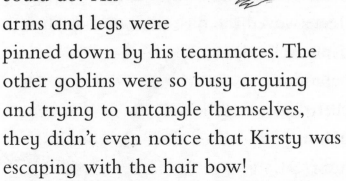

arms and legs were pinned down by his teammates. The other goblins were so busy arguing and trying to untangle themselves, they didn't even notice that Kirsty was escaping with the hair bow!

"Horrible fairies!" the goblin spat. "Always ruining our fun."

Kirsty grinned and shrugged, then she twirled up into the air with the magic bow in her arms.

Carmen zipped over to meet her.
As soon as the little fairy touched
her hair bow, it shrank down to fairy-
size. Carmen turned a series of twinkling
cartwheels in mid-air, cheering:

"We've got the bow!

And everyone will know!

Now I have to take it and go, go, go!"

She waved the girls over, and all three
of them landed
behind the
potted plant
again. With
a flick of
her wand,
Carmen
showered
Rachel and
Kirsty with

fairy dust. Just like that, they were back to their regular size!

The three friends watched as the goblins finally untangled themselves and got to their feet, rubbing their bumps and bruises. The rest of the goblins had realised that the magic hair bow was gone and they weren't happy about it! In fact, they were all so busy arguing that they completely forgot about the wedding cake. The whole group of goblins limped off down the hallway. The girls could hear them squabbling even after they'd disappeared around a corner!

"Great teamwork, girls!" Carmen said, with a big smile. "I'm heading back to Fairyland now, but I'll see you soon."

Kirsty frowned. "My competition starts

first thing in the morning. I hope we can find your magic megaphone in time!"

"Don't worry," Rachel assured her. "If we work together, I have a feeling we can save the competition."

Carmen cheered. "That's the spirit!" Then with a wink and a wave, she span up into the air and vanished.

Just then, the girls heard a loud

rumbling. Oh no – what could it be
this time?

Rachel giggled.
"I guess all that
goblin-chasing
made me
hungry. That was
my stomach!"

Kirsty linked arms
with her best friend.
"I know just the place,"
she said, leading the way
to the hotel café just off the
lobby.

When they arrived, they were greeted
with waves and friendly hellos. Kirsty's
whole squad were there! They were
seated together in a corner of the café,
snacking and chatting. Kirsty gave

Rachel a relieved smile. It looked like her team was getting along again!

"Carmen's teamwork magic is working," Kirsty whispered as the friends headed over to join Kirsty's squad.

"Just in time," Rachel said, grabbing a cookie and taking a big bite. "Mmmm magical!"

Story Three
Megaphone Madness

Chapter Eleven
Goblin Squad

"I can't believe the big competition is today," Kirsty said nervously, biting her nails as she climbed onto the shuttle bus. "It seems like we've been practising for ever!"

Rachel followed her friend down the bus aisle and plopped down in a seat next to her. "Your squad has worked so hard," she said, with a grin. "You're going to rock this!"

Kirsty gave a tiny smile. Then she sighed and peered down at her trainers.

"Hey," Rachel said, nudging Kirsty with her shoulder. "What's going on? Are you nervous?"

"Yeah, but it's more than that." Kirsty looked around the bus, frowning. "I know in my head that we're ready to compete, but I don't feel ready. And it doesn't seem like anyone else does, either!"

Rachel took in the gloomy faces of Kirsty's teammates. Kirsty was right, not a single child looked happy or excited! Where was the squad spirit?

Kirsty dropped her voice to a whisper. "What if we don't find Carmen's magic

megaphone in
time? Then
my squad
won't be able
to find our
confidence
before the
competition."

Rachel hated to see her friend so sad.
She threw an arm around Kirsty's
shoulders and flashed her a big smile.
"Then we'll just have to make sure
Carmen gets her megaphone back soon.
That's all there is to it!"

By the time the bus pulled up to the
Cove College campus, Kirsty was already
looking a little more cheerful. She couldn't
help grinning as she peeked out the
window. The outdoor venue was packed

with people! Cheerleaders milled around and warmed up quietly in different brightly coloured uniforms, while their families and friends took pictures, handed out snacks and gave pep talks. Banners and balloons hung all around the outdoor stage, and people were already filing into rows and rows of folding chairs. Upbeat music blared over a set of giant speakers. It was exactly what Kirsty had always dreamed a big cheerleading competition would be like!

Now if only Jack Frost and his goblins don't ruin it for everyone, she thought, grimly.

As everyone filed off the bus, Kirsty's teammates began chattering in low voices.

"Wow, the stage is huge!"

"People are already claiming seats!"

"Look, they're even selling T-shirts!"

Rachel and Kirsty climbed down the bus steps and looked around carefully. They knew they were supposed to let the magic find them, but the clock was ticking! Maybe they could spot a clue that would lead them to Carmen's megaphone.

Before they could even step away from

the bus, the girls heard a booming voice nearby.

"One, two, three, four; you watch us, you'll want more!"

Rachel raised an eyebrow, and Kirsty nodded. Together, they walked over to join a large crowd that had gathered on the grass. Everyone seemed to be watching a performance, but there were so many people that Rachel and Kirsty had trouble seeing through the crowd!

"Clap your hands, stomp your feet, because our squad can't be beat!"

As the same voice boomed out again, the crowd suddenly parted. The girls had a clear view of the performers jumping, cheering and clapping energetically.

"They're amazing," Kirsty said under her breath, looking gloomy.

"They're goblins!" Rachel whispered, with a gasp.

Chapter Twelve
A Pep Talk

Kirsty clapped a hand over her mouth.
"You're right!" she said. "I didn't even
recognise them in those uniforms."

Both girls stifled a giggle. The goblins
were dressed head-to-toe in matching
green cheerleading uniforms, each holding
sparkly pom-poms. They even wore green

hair bows, even though none of them had
any hair!

Rachel glanced around the crowd. "No
one seems to notice anything strange
about them," she said. In fact, the crowd
had started clapping along. The goblins'
confident energy was infectious! They
added some jumps, tumbling passes and
tosses to their routine, and no one could
deny it. They
were fantastic!

"Whoa,"
Kirsty said,
grabbing
Rachel's arm
as the goblins
completed a
tricky toss.

Rachel

sighed. "I know, they're really good."

"No! Well, yes, they are, but that's not all," Kirsty said. She dropped her voice to a whisper and pointed. "That one has Carmen's magic megaphone!"

The goblin whose voice they had heard when they got off the bus was holding a megaphone up to his mouth. When the girls looked closely, they could see that it sparkled with fairy magic!

A shiver ran up Rachel's spine. "We found it! Now we just have to get it away from the goblins before the competition starts."

111

Just then, the group of kids next to Rachel and Kirsty started talking among themselves.

"We'll never be able to beat THEM," one boy said with a groan.

Another girl nodded. "Yeah, we might as well just drop out of the competition now."

Kirsty's eyes grew wide. "We have to get that megaphone back fast," she said to Rachel. "But how? Everyone is watching the goblin squad. We can't even get close to them. It's hopeless!"

Rachel squeezed her friend's hand. "You only feel that way because the goblins have the megaphone. Everyone's confidence has vanished; mine too." She shrugged sadly. "I don't know if we can stop them this time, but we still have to try our best."

"The only thing to do is wait for them to finish performing," Kirsty said.

"Right," Rachel agreed. "Then we'll try to snag the megaphone as fast as we can and get it back to Carmen, if we can find her."

Kirsty grinned. "I think I can help with that!" She pointed behind Rachel to a nearby fountain. The water near the top of the fountain twinkled and shimmered. It almost looked like a reflection of the sunlight, but when the girls squinted, they could see a familiar tiny figure perched on the edge.

"Carmen!" Rachel cried, rushing over to the fountain with Kirsty on her heels.

The little fairy grinned up at them, kicking her feet in the trickling water.

"Hi, girls! I was hoping you'd find

me. There are so many people here!"

"People and goblins," Kirsty said, raising an eyebrow.

As the girls told Carmen all about the goblin squad, the fairy's face grew pink. She crossed her arms and huffed, "They have some nerve!" Then she looked closely at Rachel and Kirsty, who both stood with slumped shoulders. "You

seem a little down in the dumps, girls."

Rachel shrugged. "I just don't see how we're going to get your megaphone back in time, Carmen."

Carmen twirled up into the air in a burst of sparkles, then zoomed down and landed on Rachel's shoulder as quick as a wink. "Lucky for you both, I'm great at pep talks! Listen, you're only feeling like this because my megaphone isn't in Fairyland, where it should be." She fluttered her wings against Rachel's neck, and Rachel giggled. "But you two have

proven over and over that you can do anything you set your minds to!"

Kirsty and Rachel had to smile. Carmen was right!

"It's time to stop those goblins and save the competition!" Kirsty cheered.

Carmen laughed. "Now that's the spirit!"

Chapter Thirteen
An Icy Host

Luckily, the goblins finished their performance and the crowd headed off to find their seats.

Carmen tugged on Rachel's hair and pointed. "Follow those goblins!"

With some pep in her step, Rachel started after the green troublemakers but Kirsty grabbed her arm. "Wait!" she whispered, pointing to the competition stage. "This may be even trickier than we thought."

Just then, the sun disappeared behind a cloud. Rachel, Kirsty and Carmen all shivered as a tall, thin figure stepped out onto the stage, holding a megaphone up to his mouth.

"Welcome! Welcome, everyone, to the Junior Cheerleading Competition!" a familiar voice bellowed through the megaphone.

"Oh!" Rachel cried in surprise, clapping a hand over her mouth. "It's Jack Frost!"

Kirsty nodded grimly. "And he has Carmen's magic megaphone now."

Without hesitating, Carmen darted into the air. "Why, that horrible icy grouch!

I'm going to give him a
piece of my mi—"

But before Carmen
could go anywhere,
Rachel gently
grabbed her foot
between two
fingers and
held her back.
"Careful,

Carmen. You can't let the crowd spot
you!"

Carmen sighed, her wings drooping
as she slumped down on top of Rachel's
head. "You're right. I just can't stand seeing
that wicked thief with my megaphone,
especially now that the competition is
about to start!"

Up on stage, Jack Frost was still chatting

to the crowd, waving his arms
and smiling widely.
"You're going to
see some amazing
cheerleading today,
folks!"

"Yeah, from
your cheating
goblins," Kirsty
mumbled under
her breath.

"So let's get this
competition started!" Jack Frost continued.
Then, to the girls' surprise, he began
stomping his feet in rhythm and launched
into a cheer of his own!

"We're so glad you all are here,
Let's fill this stage with tons of cheer!
One, two, three, four,

The squad that wins will have the highest score!"

With that, the crowd burst into applause. Jack Frost bounced excitedly on his toes as he waved the magic megaphone over his head.

"Now if the competing squads will all assemble backstage, we'll get started in just a few minutes," Jack Frost went on after the applause died down. "Enjoy!"

Waving to the crowd, he ran offstage.

Carmen looked at the girls with wide eyes. "Well, that was strange."

"You said it," Rachel agreed. "I've never seen Jack Frost so cheerful!"

Kirsty frowned. "Your magic megaphone must be really powerful, Carmen. It's not safe with Jack Frost!"

The girls raced around to the back of the stage, with Carmen out of sight on Rachel's shoulder. But they didn't get very far before ...

BAM!

Rachel and Kirsty both ran smack into Jack Frost himself!

"Watch it!" he snapped icily. Fortunately, he barely even glanced down at them! Instead, he tossed the magic megaphone

to one of the nearby goblins. "You're up first," he called to the goblin squad. "You'd better win that trophy. It's going to be the centerpiece of the trophy case in my Ice Castle."

The girls ducked behind a set of stairs

leading up to the stage. They had to think fast!

"Hey, look!" Rachel said, pointing to where the goblin squad was gathered. "There, on the ground. Don't those look like—"

"Extra uniforms!" Kirsty cried, peering at the green clothing scattered among the goblins' messy bags.

Carmen frowned, confused. "But what good are those going to do us?"

"I have a crazy idea," Rachel said, with a grin. "And it just might work."

Chapter Fourteen
Tricks and Tumbles

With no time to waste, Rachel and Kirsty
darted out, grabbed two of the extra
goblin uniforms and ducked back behind
the stairs. They quickly changed into the
green outfits, including pom-poms. When
they were both dressed, they turned to
face Carmen.

"What do you think?" Kirsty asked the little fairy.

Carmen winked. "You're the best looking goblin cheerleaders I've ever seen! Now go get 'em!" She pointed to where the goblin squad were gathering. They were about to take the stage!

Rachel squeezed Kirsty's hand, then took a deep breath. Together, the two friends joined the group of goblins, elbowing and jostling along with the others in order to fit in.

"Look," Kirsty whispered as they all climbed on-stage. "That goblin leading the

way has Carmen's magic megaphone!"

Rachel nodded, feeling more confident now that the megaphone was so close by. "Don't let him out of your sight!"

The girls stepped on to the stage, following the goblins' lead as they jumped around excitedly, rousing the crowd. Everyone in the audience clapped and cheered as the goblins took their places.

Rachel and Kirsty stood near the back of the stage. They copied the goblins' movements as the leader's voice boomed through the magic megaphone.

"We're green, we're mean, we're a

top-notch team!"

The routine went on, and the girls followed along. All the while, they kept an eye on Carmen, who sat on the rafters above the stage. Suddenly, the little fairy waved her wand and sent a tiny stream of sparkles into the air. That was their cue!

Before the goblins knew what was happening, Kirsty was doing a perfect tumbling pass across the stage. She turned a series of cartwheels and handsprings until she reached the goblin with the megaphone, then she snatched it right out of his hand as she tumbled by!

Without hesitating, Kirsty held the megaphone to her mouth and started a cheer.

"We've got spirit, yes we do! We've got

spirit, how about you?"

The goblins all froze, looking at one another in confusion. Just then, Rachel stepped to the front of the stage and began cheering along with Kirsty, waving her

pom-poms in the air. The goblins shrugged
and followed along, trying to act like they
knew what was going on. Exactly as the
girls had hoped they would!

Kirsty continued cheering, and Rachel
gathered a group of goblins to set up a
basket toss. They quickly got into
formation. When Kirsty was done with her
cheer, the goblins lifted her up and tossed
her into the air!

As Kirsty sailed up into the air, a flash
of light flickered overhead – Carmen! The
tiny fairy darted to Kirsty and grabbed
the magic megaphone from her hand. As
soon as she touched it, the megaphone
shrank back down to fairy-size! Carmen
squealed with delight and fluttered away
before anyone could spot her.

The goblins easily caught Kirsty and

set her back down on the stage. No one even seemed to notice that she no longer had the megaphone! They worked their way through the rest of the routine and finished to a huge round of applause from the audience.

Grinning from big ear to big ear, the goblins ran off the stage, with Rachel and Kirsty trailing behind them.

Jack Frost was waiting at the bottom of the stage steps, scowling. "Not bad, not bad," he said. "Now give me that megaphone for safekeeping."

The goblins all looked around at one another, holding up empty hands.

"I don't have it!"

"I thought YOU had it!"

"Who had it last?"

"Um, it wasn't me . . ."

Rachel and Kirsty stood back, watching carefully as the goblins scrambled to cover up their mistake.

But Jack Frost wasn't amused. "You fools!" he thundered. "Do you mean to tell me you LOST the magic megaphone?"

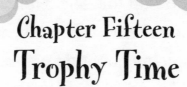

Chapter Fifteen
Trophy Time

Kirsty and Rachel froze in their tracks. They looked at each other with wide eyes.

"We can't let Jack Frost punish the goblins for this," Rachel whispered.

Kirsty paused thoughtfully. "You're right, that wouldn't be fair. Plus, if he gets really angry, he could ruin the competition with his ice magic anyway, even though Carmen has her magic objects back!"

Rachel stood up tall. She felt more confident than she had all weekend, now that the magic megaphone was back in Fairyland! "There's only one thing to do."

With that, the girls stepped forward. "Excuse me, Jack Frost?" Kirsty called.

Jack Frost's spiky head whipped around to look at the girls, and his mouth curved into a sneer. "What could you pesky girls possibly want?"

"We want to explain what happened to the magic megaphone," Rachel said calmly. "It's been returned to Fairyland by Carmen the Cheerleading Fairy."

Jack Frost's icy eyebrows shot up. "What?!" he spat. "I'll get back at that

horrible fairy for this, mark my words!"

"No, you won't," Kirsty said, with her hands on her hips. "The megaphone wasn't yours. Neither were the magic pom-poms or the magic hair bow. It's not right to take things that don't belong to you!"

A frustrated yowl came from Jack Frost's

mouth, and he raised his wand. The
goblins all cowered in fear. Rachel and
Kirsty looked at each other in panic. Now
what?

But before Jack Frost could summon any
wicked ice bolts, a sparkling light zoomed
right in front of his face. A little fairy
landed on his hand – Carmen!

"Stop!" she cried. "I have an idea that I
think you'll like, Mr Frost."

Shaking with rage, Jack Frost narrowed
his eyes. "I should send you tumbling off
my hand right now," he said to Carmen.
"But I have to admit, I'm curious. Tell me
your idea, and it had better be good!"

Carmen fluttered up into the air. "Even
better. I'll show you!"

She zipped off and returned a second
later with a huge gold trophy floating over

her head! She held her wand in the air,
using her fairy magic to move the giant
trophy along, since it was much too big
for her to carry. Then she set the trophy
down on the corner of the stage and flew

down to perch on top of it.

"I know you wanted a trophy for the case in your Ice Castle," she said. "But rather than hijacking the cheerleading trophy, I thought you might like this one better. I made it just for you!"

Jack Frost walked around the trophy slowly, examining it from every angle. Rachel and Kirsty couldn't help smiling as they watched him. The top of the huge trophy was shaped just like his spiky head!

After a few moments, Jack Frost's face

broke into a sudden grin. "I love it!" he
cried, lifting the trophy up over his head
triumphantly. "I can't wait to add it to
my trophy case." He turned to the goblins.
"Come on, team. Two, four, six, eight, time
to go, my castle awaits!" With a blast of
icy air, he and the goblins disappeared.

Carmen cartwheeled through the air,
clapping her hands. "We did it, girls! Now
the rest of the competition can go on as
planned!"

Kirsty glanced at her watch. "Speaking
of which, I need to get out of this goblin
uniform and into my own uniform; my
squad is up next!" She gave Rachel and
Carmen each a high five.

"Go get 'em, Kirsty!" Rachel cheered as
her friend ran off.

Carmen held up her wand and shot a

rainbow of magical sparkles into the air.

"I have a feeling the rest of this competition is going to be truly magical!"

The End

**Now it's time for Kirsty and
Rachel to help...**

Seren the Sausage Dog Fairy

Read on for a sneak peek...

"I think this might actually be the best
shop in the world," said Kirsty Tate.

She turned slowly on the spot, smiling
at shelves lined with pet toys, collars and
leads; tanks teeming with jewel-bright
fish; and pens filled with fluffy rabbits
and guinea pigs. Her best friend, Rachel
Walker, ran her hand over a pile of soft
puppy bedding.

"Buttons loves it in here," she said.
"Most shops don't let dogs in, but here
they always make a fuss of him."

Kirsty darted over to a display of tiny velvet cat collars.

"These would look so cute on Pearl," she said, running her fingers along the row.

Rachel crouched down to look at some dog treats. Then she shook her head and stood up again.

"I could spend hours in here," she said. "But we have to get on with our errand. Nate is relying on us."

Nate was the manager of the Leafy Lane Animal Shelter, where Rachel and Kirsty were volunteering for a few days. The shelter had rescued a litter of tiny newborn puppies, and Nate needed lots of help. He had given them a list of things to buy from the pet shop. Kirsty took it out of her pocket and read aloud.

"Five puppy collars," she said. "One pack of puppy pads, one puppy comb, one pack of puppy milk formula—"

"Not so fast!" said Rachel, who was pushing the shopping trolley. "I'm still looking at the collars."

Kirsty giggled and came over to help pick five colourful collars for the white puppies at the shelter.

"Red, yellow, pink, green and blue," she said as she dropped them in to the trolley. "They'll look like a little rainbow."

Soon the trolley was filled with puppy supplies.

"And last of all, a jumbo pack of sanitising wipes," said Rachel, adding them to the pile. "Gracious, our arms will be aching after carrying all this back to the shelter."

Just then, they heard a great commotion. People were shouting, and dogs were barking and whining.

"What on earth is going on?" Kirsty asked.

They were near the back of the shop. When they walked to the end of the aisle, they saw a big archway with the words Puppy Grooming Parlour written in curly red letters. Under the arch were three uniformed puppy groomers, swarms of puppies and a crowd of owners.

The groomers and the owners were all shouting and waving their arms around. And as for the puppies . . .

"Oh my goodness," said Kirsty, gasping.

There was a border collie whose silky coat had been curled into ringlets and decorated with at least a hundred red ribbons. A husky's coat had been gelled into spikes, and an unhappy-looking Pomeranian was modelling an 80s perm. There was a poodle whose curls had been straightened and an Afghan hound with a very wonky haircut.

"I'm so sorry," one of the groomers kept repeating. "I can't understand what's gone wrong today."

Rachel and Kirsty shared a worried

glance. They knew exactly why the puppy grooming had been such a disaster. As well as volunteering at the shelter, they had been busy helping the Puppy Care Fairies. Naughty Jack Frost had stolen their puppies, as well as the enchanted collars that helped the fairies make their magic. The girls had helped to find Li the Labrador Fairy's puppy, Buddy, and Frenchie the Bulldog Fairy's puppy, Pepper, but two of the puppies were still missing.

"Until we find Wiggles and Cleo, everything to do with grooming and training will go wrong," said Rachel.

"Look at the state of my Japanese Akita," one woman wailed at the groomers. "He's gone blue!"

"I didn't want you to shave all her fur off!" a man was complaining, holding a Bichon Frisé wrapped in a blanket.

"I wish we could help," said Kirsty.

"There's nothing we can do right now," said Rachel. "Let's go and pay."

Feeling downcast, the girls walked along the toy aisle towards the tills. As they passed a large bucket of chew toys, Kirsty stopped in her tracks.

"What is it?" Rachel asked.

Kirsty pointed at the bucket.

"That squishy octopus is glowing," she whispered.

Rachel checked left and right, but there was no one else in the aisle. Her fingers tingled with excitement as she picked up the blue octopus.

"Do you think it's magic?" she asked.

As if to answer her question, the glow grew brighter and the toy disappeared. In its place was a tiny, glimmering fairy.

"Hi, remember me?" the fairy said in a merry voice. "I'm Seren the Sausage Dog Fairy."

"Of course we do," said Rachel at once. "Welcome to Tippington."

Everything about Seren seemed bouncy and bright, from her green polka-flowered dress to her bobbed red hair. Her freckly nose scrunched up as she smiled at them.

"I'm so glad I found you," she exclaimed, jumping up and down on Rachel's hand and clapping her hands together. "I hoped and hoped that I'd find you in a quiet place so we could talk straight away."

"This isn't exactly quiet," said Kirsty, casting a nervous glance over her shoulder. "Shoppers could come down this aisle any minute."

"I'm sure they won't," said Seren. She twirled over to a nearby shelf and landed on a rubber pig toy, which let out a loud *OINK*. Seren shot upwards again and squealed with laughter.

"Wiggles would love that!" she cried.
"I have to get him one. When he comes
home, that is."

She sat down and her smile faded a
little.

"Is there still no sign of him?" asked
Rachel.

"No one has seen him," said Seren.
"But I heard a rumour, and that's why
I'm here."

"What sort of rumour?" Kirsty asked.

"I was feeling miserable this morning,"
said Seren. "I've searched everywhere,
and I've asked everyone I know, but I
haven't seen a single paw print. I was
starting to think that maybe I would

Rachel's hand and clapping her hands together. "I hoped and hoped that I'd find you in a quiet place so we could talk straight away."

"This isn't exactly quiet," said Kirsty, casting a nervous glance over her shoulder. "Shoppers could come down this aisle any minute."

"I'm sure they won't," said Seren.

She twirled over to a nearby shelf and landed on a rubber pig toy, which let out a loud *OINK*. Seren shot upwards again and squealed with laughter.

"Wiggles would love that!" she cried. "I have to get him one. When he comes home, that is."

She sat down and her smile faded.

"Is there still no sign of him?" asked Rachel.

"No one has seen him," said Seren. "But I heard a rumour, and that's why I'm here."

"What sort of rumour?" Kirsty asked.

"I was feeling miserable this morning," said Seren. "I've searched everywhere, and I've asked everyone I know, but I haven't seen a single paw print. I was starting to think that maybe I would never find Wiggles."

Rachel hopped from one foot to the other in anticipation.

"I was sitting outside my toadstool cottage when a bunny hopped up to me," Seren went on. "He was holding a never find Wiggles."

Rachel hopped from one foot to the other in anticipation.

"I was sitting outside my toadstool cottage when a bunny hopped up to me," Seren went on. "He was holding a letter in his mouth, written on a piece of bark. It was from his snow hare cousin in the Ice Mountains."

Read Seren the Sausage Dog Fairy to find out what adventures are in store for Kirsty and Rachel!

Read the brand-new series
from Daisy Meadows...

Ride. Dream. Believe.

Meet best friends Aisha and Emily
and journey to the secret world of
Enchanted Valley!

Calling all parents, carers and teachers!
The Rainbow Magic fairies are here to help
your child enter the magical world of reading.
Whatever reading stage they are at, there's
a Rainbow Magic book for everyone!
Here is Lydia the Reading Fairy's guide to
supporting your child's journey at all levels.

(1)

Starting Out
Our Rainbow Magic Beginner Readers are perfect for first-time readers who are just beginning to develop reading skills and confidence. Approved by teachers, they contain a full range of educational levelling, as well as lively full-colour illustrations.

(2)

Developing Readers
Rainbow Magic Early Readers contain longer stories and wider vocabulary for building stamina and growing confidence. These are adaptations of our most popular Rainbow Magic stories, specially developed for younger readers in conjunction with an Early Years reading consultant, with full-colour illustrations.

(3)

Going Solo
The Rainbow Magic chapter books – a mixture of series and one-off specials – contain accessible writing to encourage your child to venture into reading independently. These highly collectible and much-loved magical stories inspire a love of reading to last a lifetime.

www.orchardsseriesbooks.co.uk

"Rainbow Magic got my daughter reading chapter books. Great sparkly covers, cute fairies and traditional stories full of magic that she found impossible to put down" – Mother of Edie (6 years)

"Florence LOVES the Rainbow Magic books. She really enjoys reading now" – Mother of Florence (6 years)

Read along the Reading Rainbow!

Well done – you have completed the book!

This book was worth 2 stars.

See how far you have climbed on the Reading Rainbow opposite. The more books you read, the more stars you can colour in and the closer you will be to becoming a Royal Fairy!

Do you want to print your own Reading Rainbow?

1) Go to the Rainbow Magic website

2) Download and print out the poster

3) Colour in a star for every book you finish and climb the Reading Rainbow

4) For every step up the rainbow, you can download your very own certificate

There's all this and lots more at
orchardseriesbooks.co.uk

You'll find activities, stories, a special newsletter AND you can search for the fairy with your name!